Ricky Ricotta's

MIGHTY ROBOT

vs. THE VOODOO VULTURES FROM VENUS

STORY BY
DAV PILKEY

ART BY
DAN SANTAT

Scholastic Children's Books
An imprint of Scholastic Ltd
Euston House, 24 Eversholt Street
London, NW1 1DB, UK
Registered office: Westfield Road, Southam, Warwickshire, CV47 0RA
SCHOLASTIC and associated logos are trademarks and/or registered
trademarks of Scholastic Inc.

First published in the US by Scholastic Inc, 2001, 2014
First published in the UK by Scholastic Ltd, 2002
This edition published 2014

Text copyright © Dav Pilkey, 2001
Illustrations copyright © Dan Santat, 2014

The rights of Dav Pilkey and Dan Santat to be identified as the author and illustrator of this
work have been asserted by them.

ISBN 978 1407 14335 4

A CIP catalogue record for this book is available from the British Library.

Printed in Italy
Papers used by Scholastic Children's Books are made from wood grown in
sustainable forests.

1 3 5 7 9 10 8 6 4 2

www.scholastic.co.uk

CHAPTERS

CHAPTER ONE
LATE FOR SUPPER

It was suppertime at the Ricotta home. Ricky's father was sitting at the table. Ricky's mother was sitting at the table. But Ricky was not sitting at the table.

And neither was his Mighty Robot.

"It is six o'clock," said Ricky's father. "Ricky and his Mighty Robot are late for supper again."

Just then, Ricky and his Mighty Robot flew in.

"Sorry we are late," said Ricky. "We were in Hawaii collecting seashells."

"You have been late for supper three times this week," said Ricky's mother. "No more TV until you boys learn some responsibility."

"No TV?" cried Ricky. "But *Rocket Rodent* is on tonight. Everybody on Earth will be watching it!"

"Everybody but you two,"
said Ricky's father.

CHAPTER TWO
RESPONSIBILITY

That night, Ricky and his Mighty Robot went to bed early. They camped in the back garden under the stars.

"I wish we could watch TV tonight," said Ricky.

Ricky's Robot unscrewed his hand, and out popped a big-screen television. "No, Mighty Robot," said Ricky. "We're not allowed. We've got to learn some responsibility first."

Ricky's Mighty Robot did not know what *responsibility* was.

"*Responsibility*," said Ricky, "is doing the right thing at the right time."

Ricky and his Mighty Robot were pretty good at doing the right thing . . .

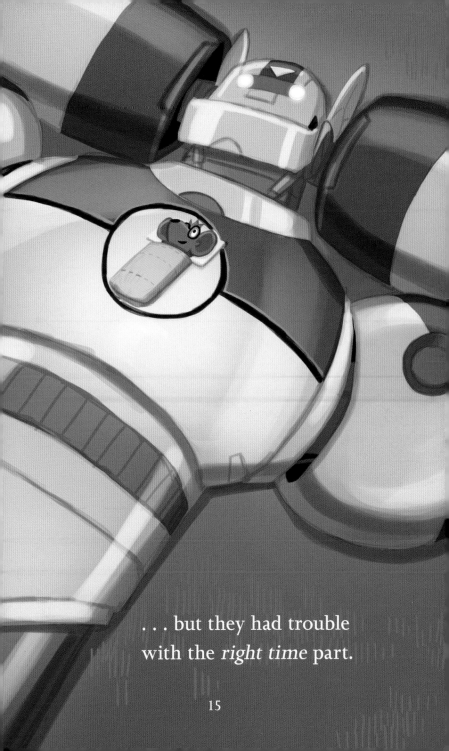

. . . but they had trouble
with the *right time* part.

CHAPTER THREE
VICTOR VON VULTURE

At that very moment, over forty million kilometres away, there lived an evil vulture on the planet Venus.

TEMPERATURE: 864 DEGREES

ONLY 2,915 HOURS TILL SUNSET!

TODAY'S FORECAST:
MOSTLY GASSY
(WITH A CHANCE OF
SULPHURIC ACID).

His name was Victor Von Vulture,
and he hated living on Venus.

It was so hot on Venus that everyone's food was always ruined. Their grilled cheese sandwiches were always *way too gooey* . . .

. . . they had to drink their chocolate
bars with straws . . .

. . . and everybody's ice cream melted before they could even get one lick!

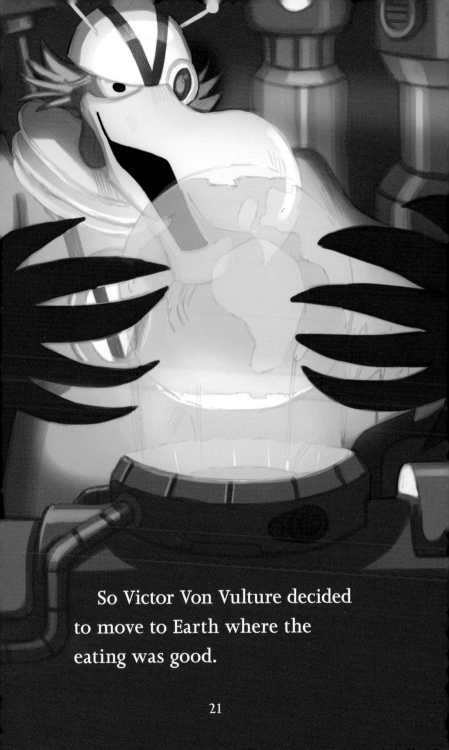

So Victor Von Vulture decided
to move to Earth where the
eating was good.

First, he invented the Voodoo-Schmoodoo 2000. Then he climbed aboard and went looking for an army.

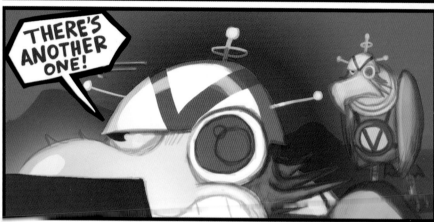

VICTOR VON VULTURE HAD HIS ARMY.

NOW I NEED A BIG ARMY!

SECRET GROWTH RAY
CLICK

GZZZZZZZZZZ

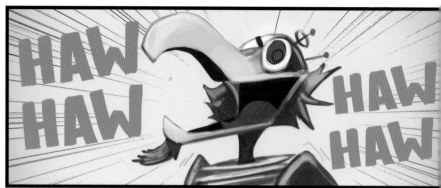

CHAPTER FOUR
VOODOO RAYS
FROM OUTER SPACE

Ricky and his Mighty Robot fell asleep under the stars, while everyone else in town was watching television.

Suddenly, a voodoo ray from outer space beamed down through the night sky. The strange signal was picked up by all the TVs in town.

The screens began to glow eerily as a strange voice came from the wicked signal.

"Obey the Voodoo Vultures!" said the voice. "Obey the Voodoo Vultures!"

Soon, every mouse in the city
was hypnotized.

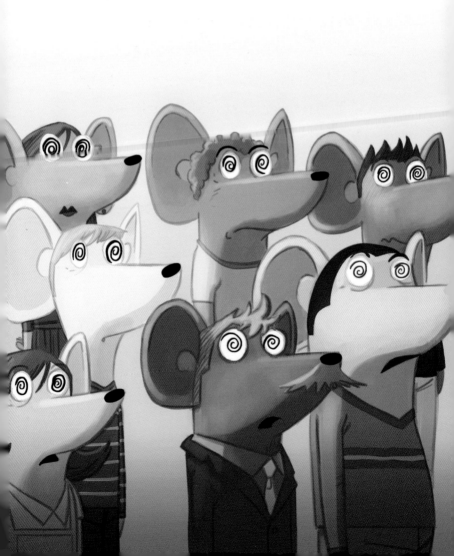

CHAPTER FIVE
BREAKFAST WITH THE ROBOT

The next morning, Ricky woke up and went inside to fix breakfast. But all the food in the house was gone.

"Hey!" said Ricky. "Where's all the food? I can't go to school without breakfast!"

Ricky's Robot knew just what to do. He flew straight to Florida. A few seconds later, he returned with an orange tree.

"Thanks, Mighty Robot," said Ricky. "I love freshly squeezed orange juice! Now, may I have a doughnut?"

Ricky's Mighty Robot flew off again. Soon he returned with some fresh doughnuts.

"Hey!" Ricky laughed. "I said *a* doughnut . . .
not a doughnut *store*! Please put that
back and bring me some milk!"

Ricky's Robot flew away again. This time he returned with the freshest milk he could find.

"Ummm. . ." said Ricky. "I think I'll skip the milk today!"

CHAPTER SIX
OBEY THE VOODOO VULTURES

After breakfast, the Mighty Robot
flew Ricky straight to school. But
something was not right!

All the mice in school had strange looks on their faces.

They were all carrying food out of the cafeteria door, straight to the centre of town.

Ricky found his reading teacher, Miss Swiss.

"What's going on here?" asked Ricky.
"Obey the Voodoo Vultures," said
Miss Swiss.

Then Ricky saw his maths teacher, Mr Mozzarella.

"Aren't we supposed to have a test today?" asked Ricky.

"Obey the Voodoo Vultures," said Mr Mozzarella.

Finally, Ricky found Principal Provolone.

"Where is everybody going with all this food?" asked Ricky.

"Obey the Voodoo Vultures," said Principal Provolone.

Ricky was not getting any answers.
"Come on, Robot," said Ricky. "We've
got to get to the bottom of this!"

CHAPTER SEVEN
THOSE VICIOUS VULTURES

Ricky and his Mighty Robot followed
the long line of mice to the centre of
town. There, they saw a horrible sight!

Victor Von Vulture had taken over the city and turned everybody into voodoo slaves. The hungry Vultures were eating every bite of food in town.

"We want more chocolate chip cookies!" yelled one of the Vultures.

"Yesss, Masters," said the mice as they scurried off to start baking.

"And no more *rice cakes*!" yelled another Vulture.

"We've got to stop those evil Vultures,"
Ricky whispered. "But how?"

Ricky and his Mighty Robot looked
around. They saw Victor and his evil
invention.

"I'll bet those Vultures are controlling everybody with that remote control," said Ricky. "We've got to get it away from them." But that was going to be tricky.

"Hmmm," said Ricky. "What we need is a *distraction*."

CHAPTER EIGHT
RICKY'S RECIPE

Ricky and his Mighty Robot hurried back to school. In the cafeteria kitchen, Ricky mixed together some butter, sugar, and eggs. Then he added flour and chocolate chips.

"Now comes the secret ingredient," said Ricky.

The Mighty Robot flew straight
to Mexico and returned with the
hottest peppers he could find.

Ricky stirred the cookie batter while his Mighty Robot added hundreds of super red-hot chilli peppers to the mix.

The Mighty Robot quickly baked
the cookies with his microwave
eyeballs, then cooled the pan with
his super-freezy breath.

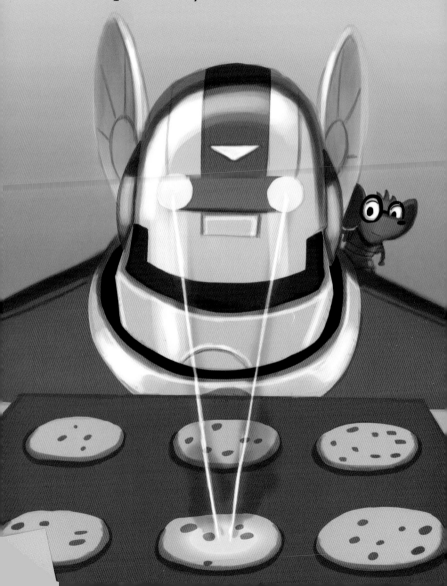

CHAPTER NINE
DINNER IS SERVED

Ricky and his Mighty Robot returned to the centre of town. Ricky pretended he was hypnotized as he bravely carried his cookies towards the Voodoo Vultures.

"It's about time!" said one of the Vultures.
"Gimme those cookies!" said another.
The greedy Vultures were fighting over Ricky's cookies. They stuffed them into their mouths as fast as they could.

"OUCHIE! OUCHIE! *OUCHIE!*" screamed
the Vultures as they danced around in pain.

Ricky's Mighty Robot grabbed the Voodoo-Schmoodoo 2000 and crushed it in his mighty fist.

Suddenly, all the mice in town returned to normal. They screamed at the sight of the Voodoo Vultures, and everybody ran straight home. Ricky's Mighty Robot had saved the city . . . but Victor Von Vulture had another plan.

CHAPTER TEN
RICKY'S BRIGHT IDEA

Victor Von Vulture knew that Ricky
and the Mighty Robot were working
together. Quickly, he swooped down
and grabbed Ricky. "Don't come any
closer, Mighty Robot," said Victor,
"or I will destroy your little friend!"

The Voodoo Vultures were very angry. They huffed and they puffed as they surrounded Ricky's Mighty Robot.

"You're going to be sorry you tricked us!" said Victor Von Vulture as he flew higher and higher.

Just when everything seemed
hopeless, Ricky had an idea.

He reached up and grabbed a feather
from Victor Von Vulture's rear end.
Ricky yanked the feather out.

"Ouch!" yelled Victor.

Ricky wiggled the feather
under Victor's claw.

"H-Hey! S-S-Stop that! It tickles!" laughed Victor Von Vulture.

But Ricky did not stop. He wiggled the feather faster and faster. Victor began laughing harder and harder.

Finally, Victor Von Vulture let
go of Ricky. The little mouse fell
through the air. . .

CHAPTER ELEVEN

ROBO-RESCUE

Ricky was in big trouble. He was falling through the sky, faster and faster. "Help me, Mighty Robot!" Ricky cried.

With lightning speed, the Mighty
Robot's arm shot up into the air. The
Mighty Robot caught Ricky by the
back of his shirt . . .

. . . and set him down safely in a tree.

"Thanks, buddy," said Ricky. "Now
go get 'em!"

CHAPTER TWELVE
THE BATTLE BEGINS

The Mighty Robot flew up and grabbed Victor in his mighty fist.

"Help, Voodoo Vultures, HELP!!!" yelled Victor.

Suddenly, the evil Voodoo Vultures
got ready to attack. The Mighty Robot
was outnumbered.

"This is going to be fun," Victor snarled.

The Voodoo Vultures began to attack.
The Mighty Robot defended himself.

"Hey, wait a minute, Robot," said Victor. "Put me down first!"

But the Mighty Robot did not have time to put Victor down. Victor was stuck in the middle of the fight.

Every time the Mighty Robot
punched, Victor felt the blow!

Every time the Mighty Robot clobbered,
Victor got clobbered, too!

Every time the Mighty Robot clunked
heads, Victor got the worst of it!

"Ouchie, ouchie, *ouchie*!" cried Victor Von Vulture. "This is not as much fun as I thought it would be!"

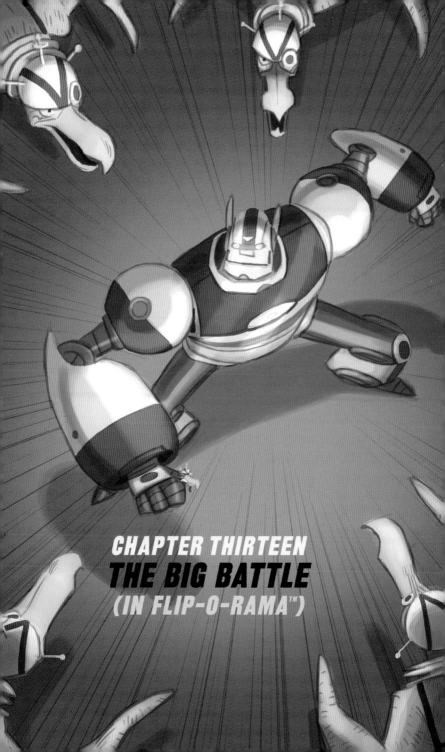

CHAPTER THIRTEEN
THE BIG BATTLE
(IN FLIP-O-RAMA™)

-RAMA

HERE'S HOW IT WORKS!

STEP 1

Place your *left* hand inside the dotted lines marked "LEFT HAND HERE". Hold the book open *flat*.

STEP 2

Grasp the *right-hand* page with your right thumb and index finger (inside the dotted lines marked "RIGHT THUMB HERE").

STEP 3

Now *quickly* flip the right-hand page back and forth until the picture appears to be *animated*.

(For extra fun, try adding your own sound-effects!)

FLIP-O-RAMA 1

(pages 95 and 97)

Remember, flip *only* page 95.
While you are flipping, be sure you
can see the picture on page 95
and the one on page 97.
If you flip quickly, the two
pictures will start to look like
<u>one</u> *animated* picture.

Don't forget to add
your own sound-effects!

LEFT HAND HERE

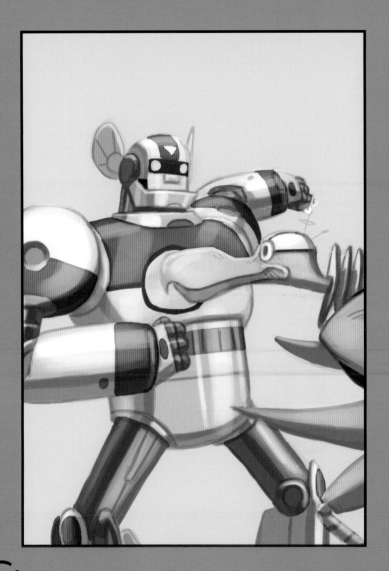

THE VOODOO VULTURES ATTACKED.

RIGHT
THUMB
HERE

RIGHT
INDEX
FINGER
HERE

96

**THE VOODOO
VULTURES ATTACKED.**

FLIP-O-RAMA 2

(pages 99 and 101)

Remember, flip *only* page 99.
While you are flipping, be sure you
can see the picture on page 99
and the one on page 101.
If you flip quickly, the two
pictures will start to look like
<u>one</u> *animated* picture.

Don't forget to add
your own sound-effects!

LEFT HAND HERE

RICKY'S ROBOT
FOUGHT BACK.

RIGHT
THUMB
HERE

**RICKY'S ROBOT
FOUGHT BACK.**

FLIP-O-RAMA 3
(pages 103 and 105)

Remember, flip *only* page 103.
While you are flipping, be sure you
can see the picture on page 103
and the one on page 105.
If you flip quickly, the two
pictures will start to look like
<u>one</u> *animated* picture.

Don't forget to add
your own sound-effects!

LEFT HAND HERE

THE VOODOO VULTURES BATTLED HARD.

103

RIGHT
THUMB
HERE

104

**THE VOODOO VULTURES
BATTLED HARD.**

FLIP-O-RAMA 4

(pages 107 and 109)

Remember, flip *only* page 107.
While you are flipping, be sure you
can see the picture on page 107
and the one on page 109.
If you flip quickly, the two
pictures will start to look like
<u>one</u> *animated* picture.

Don't forget to add
your own sound-effects!

LEFT HAND HERE

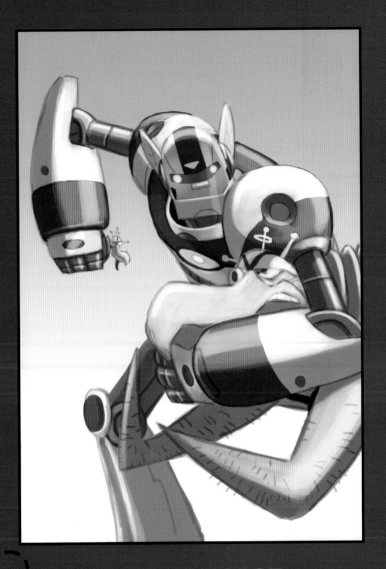

RICKY'S ROBOT
BATTLED HARDER.

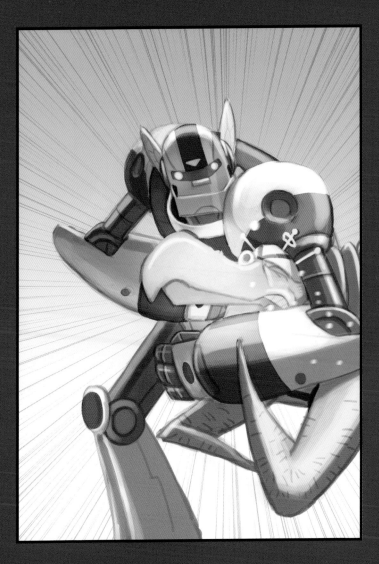

RICKY'S ROBOT
BATTLED HARDER.

FLIP-O-RAMA 5

(pages 111 and 113)

Remember, flip *only* page 111.
While you are flipping, be sure you
can see the picture on page 111
and the one on page 113.
If you flip quickly, the two
pictures will start to look like
<u>one</u> *animated* picture.

Don't forget to add
your own sound-effects!

LEFT HAND HERE

AND JUSTICE PREVAILED.

111

RIGHT
THUMB
HERE

RIGHT
INDEX
FINGER
HERE

112

AND JUSTICE PREVAILED.

CHAPTER FOURTEEN
JUSTICE PREVAILS

The evil Voodoo Vultures were no
match for Ricky Ricotta's Mighty Robot.
"Let's get out of here!" moaned the
Vultures.

"Hey, wait for *ME!*"
cried Victor Von Vulture.
But it was too late.
The Voodoo Vultures flew back to
Venus and were never heard from again.

The Mighty Robot picked up Ricky, and together they took Victor Von Vulture to the Squeakyville prison.

"Boo-hoo-hoo!" cried Victor.
"Maybe now you will learn some responsibility!" said Ricky.

Then Ricky Ricotta and his Mighty
Robot flew straight home . . .

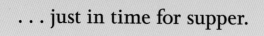

. . . just in time for supper.

CHAPTER FIFTEEN
SUPPERTIME

Ricky's mother and father had cooked a wonderful feast for Ricky and his Mighty Robot.

"Oh, boy!" said Ricky. "TV dinners! My favourite!"

"We're both very proud of you boys," said Ricky's mother.

"Thank you for doing the right thing at the right time," said Ricky's father.

"No problem," said Ricky . . .

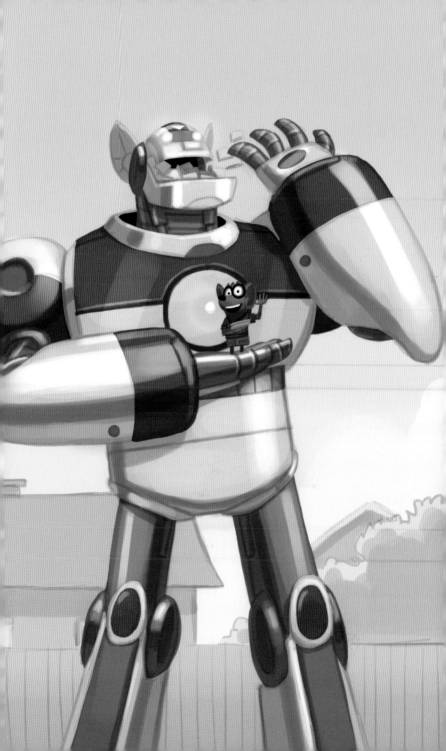

. . . "that's what friends are for!"

READY FOR

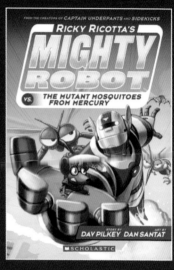

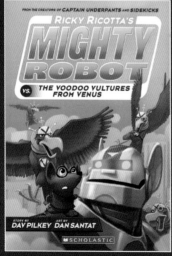

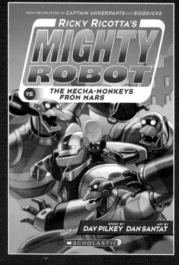

MORE RICKY?

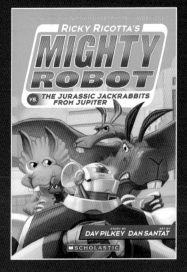

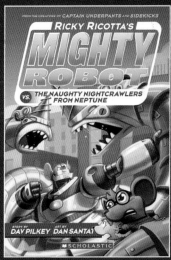

DAV PILKEY

has written and illustrated more than fifty books for children, including *The Paperboy*, a Caldecott Honor book; *Dog Breath: The Horrible Trouble with Hally Tosis*, winner of the California Young Reader Medal; and the IRA Children's Choice *Dumb Bunnies* series. He is also the creator of the *New York Times* best-selling *Captain Underpants* books. Dav lives in the Pacific Northwest with his wife. Find him online at www.pilkey.com.

DAN SANTAT

is the writer and illustrator of the picture book *The Adventures of Beekle: The Unimaginary Friend*. He is also the creator of the graphic novel *Sidekicks* and has illustrated many acclaimed picture books, including the *New York Times* bestseller *Because I'm Your Dad* by Ahmet Zappa and *Crankenstein* by Samantha Berger. Dan also created the Disney animated hit *The Replacements*. He lives in Southern California with his family. Find him online at www.dantat.com.